A FALLEN
WARLORD

A Fallen Warlord

ISBN-10: 1-9459-9406-1
ISBN-13: 978-1-9459-9406-7

edited by Jessica Johnson
interior artwork by Rachel Fast

Cover art by Vuk Kostic (Chevsy on DeviantArt.com)
licensed through DepositPhoto.com

Tannhauser Press

This is a work of fiction. All characters and events portrayed in this story are fictitious. Any resemblance to an actual goblin attack is purely coincidental.

To my niece Marlene

who knows more about Tolkien's world
than anyone I've ever met

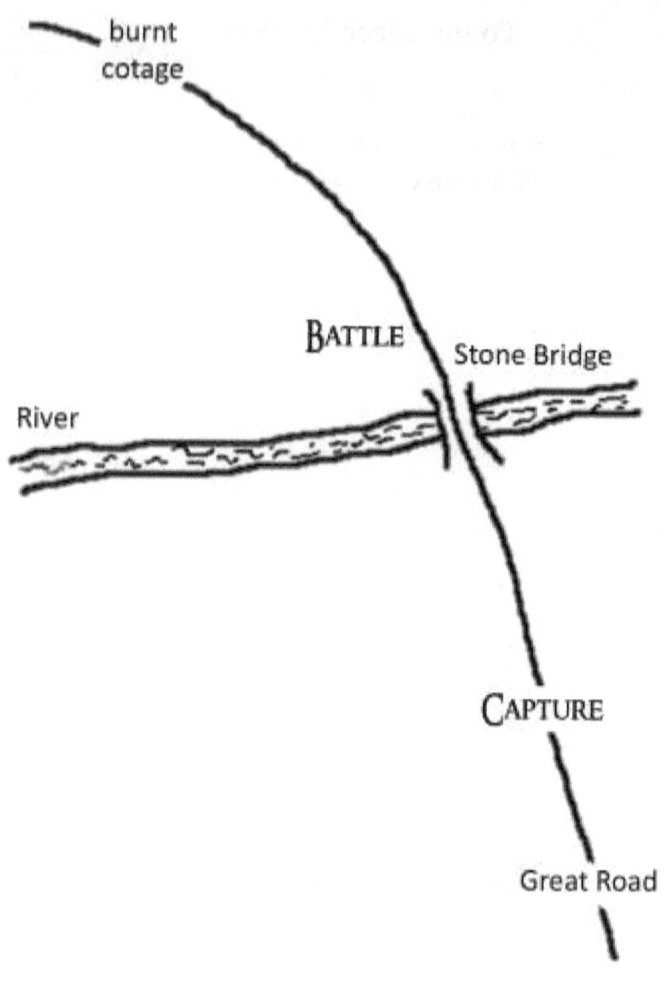

burnt
cotage

BATTLE

Stone Bridge

River

CAPTURE

Great Road

The Site of the Battle

Prologue

ord Zuriel, you are a coward!" General Olwen shook his fist at the backs of the fleeing horsemen.

Half a dozen riders, all in black, fled before the General. A banner bearing the enemy warlord's device, the symbol for earth twisted into the symbol for fire, streamed above their heads, and hoofbeats shook the ground.

The largest of the horsemen reined in and turned to face the General.

"What did you call me?" His voice was low and harsh. He spurred his black stallion forward, and his sword came out of the scabbard with a hiss. Behind him, his companions melted into the chaos of the rout, unaware their leader was no longer with them.

General Olwen sat in the saddle, the reins loose in his hands. He made no move for the hilt of his own sword.

"You flatter yourself if you think I'd duel with you as an equal. You're nothing but a thug with an army.

Beneath the helm, the warlord's mouth twisted in contempt. "I will annihilate you." He advanced with the confidence of one who has an army at his back.

The horses of the General's men danced around, whinnying, and their riders fought for control. Only the General's mount remained still, beyond a twitch that rippled up its haunches.

"Look behind you," said the General.

1

The warlord hesitated, then turned to look over his shoulder. Shields and weapons littered the ground where his people had dropped them. Other than that, the road was empty. So were the surrounding fields. The warlord's arm froze in mid-gesture.

General Olwen laughed, then nodded to one of his lieutenants. "Take him."

A dozen foot soldiers pulled the sorcerer warlord from the saddle.

The General's stallion danced sideways and showed the whites of its eyes. The horses of his captains tossed their heads and reared up. One of them almost threw its rider.

"Sir, we can barely control the horses," said the General's second-in-command. "Something's not right."

Chapter 1

Outermost Island

alwin waded into the chilly surf. He gasped as the water hit his skin. Midwinter's day was weeks away, and the sea was wintery cold. The young islander picked his way over the rocks. They were sharp beneath his feet and so slippery, he had to work to keep his footing.

The waves crested and then slid out again, the foaming brine cutting white channels between the boulders. He'd rolled up his leggings, but the incoming surf slid past his ankles, the calves of his legs, and above his knees. Seawater soaked into the often-patched fabric.

Cliffs pressed in on three sides of the little cove. A footpath led between the sea grasses to the plateau that formed most of the island. Outermost Island, home to ten families, was little more than a rock sticking out of the ocean, the northern tip of a chain of islands which formed the Island Kingdom of Armelos.

To the south, the profile of their nearest neighbor rose from the sea. Behind it, a larger island could just be seen on the line where sea met sky, grey and indistinct.

To the north, the horizon was empty except for the purple-blue sea and the endless sky.

Halwin lifted the heavy net and shook it a few times to untangle it. He spoke a charm to summon the fish and cast it on foaming surf. The weighted corners sank, leaving only the billowy center. The waves retreated, and he pulled in the net.

A few undersized silver fish wriggled in the latticework of knotted cords. The largest was a hand span in length. The others were no bigger than his thumb. Halwin's shoulders slumped. When he was a boy, his father used to pull in nets flopping with silver fish. But this was his best haul after casting the net all morning. He untangled them and dropped them in the bucket.

Like everyone else on the island, his family relied on the sea for food. They also grew turnips and carrots in their gardens, hollows in the rock filled with dirt from the seaweed they carried up, but what they grew in their small plots wasn't enough to live on.

Discouraged, Halwin decided he'd fished enough for one day. The surf hissed up the beach and then retreated, leaving an armload of kelp on the coarse sand. With a sigh, he bent to gather it up. *You can never have too much dead kelp.*

The slimy ribbons were cold against his skin and soaked the front of his smock. He dropped them into the basket he'd brought along for the purpose and went back for more.

A pebble poked out of the sand, round with a streak of orange through the quartz. He picked it up and rolled it in his fingers. It was too nice to throw away, so he put it in his pocket.

"Halwin!"

Cuinn, his closest friend, stood at the top of the footpath leading down to the cove. Cuinn was young, but already there were strands of silver in his black hair and his back was stooped from bending over the hoe and pulling in the nets.

"What is it?" Halwin asked.

"There's a gigantic ship to the south, larger than any I've ever seen." His round face, usually open and untroubled, was pinched with anxiety.

Halwin tucked the bucket of fish in with the kelp, then lifted the basket with both hands. He headed up the slope, wishing he had a hand free to grasp the edge of the path for balance. Succulent plants covered the ground and held the sand in place. At the top, the land leveled out to a flat rocky plain.

Cuinn stood on the plateau, looking out to sea. Fine lines marred the corners of his eyes.

"There, midway between us and the next island over," said Cuinn.

Halwin looked where his friend was pointing. In the middle distance, the outline of an enormous ship emerged from the mist. It wasn't a fishing boat, at least not one from this island or any nearby. A small house had been built on its foredeck and a larger one on its stern. As they watched, sailors moved around on the roofs.

"It looks like it's coming here," said Cuinn. "Let's go to the harbor for a better look."

Halwin dumped the kelp into a hollow of rock next to the last load he'd brought up. He left the bucket of fish in the door of his family's cottage and went racing after Cuinn.

The ship was closer now. From the cliff above the pier, a dozen men were visible on deck, and there were more in the rigging. On the next tack, the vessel caught a breeze and heeled over, cutting through the water at the head of a foaming wake.

"I've never seen a fishing boat move that fast," said Cuinn. "You don't suppose they're pirates?"

The island had no way to defend itself beyond what able-bodied men with scythes and flails could do. Most of those men were out on fishing boats at the moment.

"This can't be happening." Cuinn gripped Halwin's arm. His voice was tight.

Halwin shaded his eyes and squinted. The deep blue mainsail bore some sort of emblem, a ship with a crown above it. Halwin recognized it and sagged with relief.

"I don't think we need to worry. That's the Royal badge of Armelos," he said.

The vessel tacked again, setting a course that took it into the entrance of their little bay. It lowered its sails and dropped anchor.

"Let's go down to the pier to meet them," said Halwin.

Halwin hurried across the island, with Cuinn right behind him. They climbed down the stone steps carved into the hillside that led to a long plank dock. The tide was out, exposing tall pilings encrusted with barnacles. By late afternoon, half a dozen fishing boats would tie up here when they came in from the sea, but at the moment, there wasn't a fishing boat in sight.

However, the dock itself was packed to overflowing with people looking out to sea, and more people climbed the rocks on shore, squinting and shading their eyes. Halwin stopped before he reached the bottom of the stairs. He could see as well from there as anywhere else.

As they watched the strange vessel approach, the crowd buzzed with talk. Even the oldest among them said a ship that size had never visited the island before.

In the middle of the bay, sailors on the huge vessel lowered a longboat to the water. Three men climbed down the side of the ship and jumped into the longboat. Two men rowed, and the third sat astern, on the thwart. The launch approached the end of the pier, and one of the oarsmen dropped the painter over a piling. The passenger stood. The dock came to his chest, but he let the swell lift him and climbed up as easily as any sailor.

The man didn't look like a sailor. His robes fell below his knee. They were made from a rich fabric, and he wore a sword at his belt. He must be a great lord. Halwin had never seen a nobleman before. He looked away, suddenly shy.

The visitor raised his hand, and the crowd fell silent. "Citizens of Armelos, I am Lord Gavin, a lieutenant in the King's army." He spoke the language of the Capital. Halwin had to translate in his head, and he struggled to keep up.

"A rogue warlord came out of the east swept across the Mainland," said the Lieutenant. "He captured the region where most of our grain is grown. This coming fall, there will be famine. The wheat, oats, and barley you rely on will vanish from the marketplace. You'll have to live on whatever you can catch."

"We'll starve!" someone wailed.

"May the Gods help us!" cried another.

The man held up a hand for silence. "Lord Zuriel may have seized those lands, but he won't hold them. We're going to drive him out."

A murmuring passed through the crowd. Lieutenant Gavin waited for it to die down before he continued speaking.

"The King needs soldiers. As a soldier, you'll earn a handsome wage, and you'll get a substantial bonus when you sign on. But you must decide quickly. We sail at the turn of tide."

Chapter 2

The Great Ship

The Lieutenant opened a ledger and set it on top of a piling. A young man approached and spoke to him, then bent down to sign it. Two other youths stood nearby, listening. Halwin watched with interest, even though he had no interest in joining the army himself.

The crowd began to break up. Halwin followed his neighbors up the stone steps to the top of the cliff. "It sounds exciting, but it's not for me," said Halwin.

Beside him, Cuinn was unusually quiet.

"I don't expect it's for you, either," Halwin said. "You have a little one on the way."

"That bonus. It's a lot of money," Cuinn said.

From the plateau, they watched as the longboat, looking like a toy at this distance, returned to the great ship anchored in the harbor. Men moved around on the decks, and one or two climbed into the rigging.

Outside his own cottage, Halwin knelt to pluck a sprig of rosemary and a sprig of sage from the dried stems from last summer's kitchen garden.

The building was a single long room with a fireplace at one end. A space at the far end was screened off for a tiny bedchamber, its ceiling forming the floor of a sleeping loft Halwin shared with his nieces and nephews.

Inside, the room smelled of wood smoke from driftwood burning in the hearth. Halwin's sister-in-law lifted the lid of an iron kettle. The aroma of peas porridge filled the small space. Children raced around, shrieking like fiends over possession of the cat.

Halwin knelt at the hearth. He twisted the sprigs together and laid them in the fire. Tendrils of fragrant smoke rose from the coals. He said a prayer for his friends who would leave to fight in the war. The smoke would carry his words to the Gods, or in polite language, the Holy One, the spirits who move among unseen among ordinary people. Halwin felt closest to the spirits of Water and favored them in his prayers. The spirits of Earth or Air or Fire could hear his prayers too, but he felt he didn't know them as well.

Halwin's older brother appeared in the doorway, exhausted from a day on the water. Pulling cold, soaking nets onto a heaving deck was no one's idea of easy work. He wasn't carrying any fish. More and more, the bad days outnumbered the good.

Halwin's sister-in-law called them to the table. She spooned a thick porridge of dried peas and barley into bowls. Halwin took a bite. There was no fish in it. Porridge without fish had no staying power. He'd be hungry before bedtime.

There should be fish for supper tonight, at least a few bites. He'd caught a few this morning. Halwin stiffened. He'd left the bucket in the doorway to the cottage, unwatched. He glared at the cat. It met his gaze with a look, "Prove it."

"What happened to the fish I caught?" Halwin asked.

His brother looked embarrassed. "The rudder pin snapped. Your three fish bought us a new one."

"Aren't rudder pins expensive?" asked Halwin.

"Aye. But as long as folks are pulling in empty nets, even the smallest fish will fetch a handful of coins."

They ate in silence. Halwin snuck a finger-full of porridge to the dog, and his sister-in-law pretended not to notice. They talked about the poor fish harvest. It was the worst problem Halwin had ever faced, and he didn't see how could be solved. He changed the subject. "Did you see the ship in the bay? They've come to recruit soldiers for a war on the Mainland."

His brother asked, "Will you sign up?"

"No. You need me here. I have to cast the net and collect kelp to expand the garden. I can't leave you."

"The King needs you, too," said his brother.

Halwin avoided his brother's eye. He felt like he was shirking his duty. But what did Halwin owe the crown? He knew nothing of King Turstan beyond his name.

When supper was over, Halwin escaped to Cuinn's cottage next door. Hours had passed since they'd left the dock where the Lieutenant spoke about the war, but they hadn't had a chance to talk about it. The footpath between their houses had worn into a deep trench. It had been that way since before he was born.

The door to Cuinn's house stood open. Halwin stepped inside. The small dwelling was laid out exactly like Halwin's, but if Halwin's was crowded, his closest friend's was more so. Cuinn was one of seven brothers and sisters. The oldest three were married with children of their own. However, since there was nowhere for them to go, they still lived with their parents.

On the far side of the room, Cuinn and his wife were huddled in conversation. Cuinn whispered intensely and gestured with his hands, which wasn't like him. They seemed to reach a decision Cuinn got up and stood in front of the mantelpiece, then draped his arm over his wife's shoulders. Beneath her apron, her belly was as round as an iron kettle.

"Hear me." Cuinn raised his voice to carry over the din. People in every corner of the room stopped what they were doing and fell silent. "I've decided to enlist. The sign-on bonus and the wages paid to a soldier will let us buy a farm of our own."

Cuinn's father looked grim, and his mother burst into tears. Cuinn's oldest brother, who would inherit the farm one day, leaned against the door jamb, his face grave. Children playing on the hard-packed floor appeared to be absorbed in their game, but Halwin saw a child's hand hang motionless over a toy sheep.

Halwin stormed out, too angry to speak. Back at his own house, he sat on the floor and wrapped his arms wrapped around the neck of his dog. Its soft fur smelled of wet collie and the discarded parts of fish. *How could he? How could he just leave us?* There was a knock on the door. A childish voice called out, "Cuinn's leaving now. Come say farewell."

Reluctantly, Halwin got to his feet and went outside. Next door, Cuinn stood in front of his family's cottage with a bundle over his shoulder. He was saying goodbye to his wife, who couldn't manage the steps down to the pier. Cuinn turned to go, and the rest of the hamlet followed to see him off. Halwin trailed behind them, still too angry to be civil.

They descended the stairs to the base of the cliff and walked onto the dock. Almost every young man on the island waited there with a bundle or a wooden chest at his feet. At the end of the dock, three longboats floated almost level with the wooden planks.

The sea had risen almost to the underside of the dock, and the barnacled pilings were completely concealed. The tide was fully in and about to turn. It was time to go.

"Into the boats, men," said Lieutenant Gavin.

Halwin's friends and neighbors climbed into the longboats. The oarsmen cast off, and the first two boats rowed away. The new recruits waved to the islanders staying behind, then looked ahead to the great warship bobbing at anchor.

Cuinn joined the others in the remaining longboat. A sailor started to untie the painter. Cuinn waved goodbye, his face set with quiet resolve.

"Wait! I'm coming too!" Halwin grabbed the pen to sign, accepted a purse of coins and shoved it in his brother's hands, and stepped into the boat beside Cuinn.

The sailor cast off and began to row. Halwin turned and looked at the pier. His family started back at him, stunned. "I'm off to war!" he shouted across the widening gap between boat and dock.

Chapter 3 The Voyage South

oon they were crossing the middle of the harbor, gliding over the kelp beds. The hull of the longboat hissed over the rubbery weeds. The water was unnaturally warm here, and noxious bubbles broke on the surface.

In the kelp forest deep below, the nymphs waited for them, their faces grey as drowned flesh and their hair floating like seaweed. Their clammy fingers could seize a man's ankle and pull him into the depths. Halwin spoke a charm to ward them off, then said to the oarsman, "We should avoid this place. It's not wise to disturb the nymphs." A fellow islander who'd been trailing his fingers in the water yanked back his hand.

"You do know that nymphs are a superstition?" asked Lieutenant Gavin, looking amused.

The Lieutenant was from the Capital. Like many city people, it appeared that he'd lost the old knowledge. Halwin said nothing, but he knew the supernatural was all around them and should be treated with respect.

The longboat bumped against the side of the great ship. "Here we are, men. Climb up," said the Lieutenant. One at a time, they stood up in the small boat and scrambled up the boards nailed into the hull which formed the rungs of a ladder.

The ship was full of young men from the neighboring islands. Halwin already knew some of them, like Alaric, a slender red-headed youth a year younger than himself, and

Ulrich, a giant of a man who solved all his problems with his fists.

Most of the others were strangers to him. Halwin made and effort to talk to the ones he didn't know, and to learn their names and faces. Brennan was a spotty-faced youth with hair the color of harness leather, and Hador, a silent and watchful version of Ulrich.

Halwin stood at the rail and watched as the prow lifted and dropped on the waves. Someone had tied a bundle of sweet smelling herbs to the bowsprit, an offering to the spirits who lived in the sea. With each swell, they dipped below the surface and rose again, the water streaming off it. Halwin nodded in satisfaction. At least the sailors still kept to the old ways, even if people like the Lieutenant didn't.

They sailed south. They left Outermost Island in their wake, and one by one, each the islands to the south. Each was larger and had more people than the one before. The ship didn't stop at any of them, but stayed in blue water, well out to sea. "We have to give the shallows a wide berth," said one of the sailors. "A warship this size draws at least two fathoms, and could easily run aground."

Late in the afternoon, they glided past the largest of the outer islands, a long shelf of rock clothed in green fields and small stands of trees. At one point, Halwin could see to the back of the harbor where a town spread out behind the pier. Town, not village.

A town was home to people who did more than farm or fish for a living. They made things other people couldn't make for themselves, like blades for hoes or barrels that didn't leak.

Above the high tide line, white awnings sparkled in the sun and crowds pressed around them. It must be market day. Halwin watched with longing. He traveled here to go to the market whenever he could, as much as two or three times a year. He'd gladly go more often, but in a small fishing boat, it took the better part of a day to get here.

Halwin remembered the last time he'd come to the island for the market, the previous fall. Even from the water, the sight of white linen stretched over frames revealed that something exciting was happening in town. He hurried down the pier and pushed his way through the tightly packed crowd.

Under the awnings, merchants displayed their wares on makeshift tables of planks balanced on sawhorses or the tops of barrels.

At the market, one could buy things that didn't grow in the rocky soil of Outermost Island. Whenever he came here, Halwin always brought home a dozen sacks of grain, three or four each of barley, wheat, and oats. Most of the coarse hempen bags were stenciled with foreign symbols, showing they'd come all the way from the Mainland. It made an ordinary object, like a burlap bag, interesting and exotic.

Halwin stopped in his tracks. If they failed to drive off the warlord, there might not be any grain for sale next fall.

But for now, the merchants' stalls were busy and prosperous. Other booths sold eggs, fresh fruit, butter, and cheese. If someone needed a chicken or a goat, they could find one here, too.

Once Halwin needed a pair of oarlocks, and the blacksmith made them for him while he watched. There were luxury goods as well, like writing paper, leather shoes, and wool that had already been woven into cloth or even sewn into clothing. On his most recent trip here last fall, one of the merchants had a booth full of things a young man might give to a girl he liked, like silk hair ribbons or a small leather purse. Halwin picked up a silver chain and turned it over in his hand.

"That would look good on your sweetheart," said the merchant.

With a stab, Halwin realized he didn't know any girls. Reluctantly, he put it back.

The great ship moved on and left the market town behind. Fields and farmland slipped away behind their stern and disappeared behind the horizon.

"Where are we going?" Halwin asked one of the sailors.

"We're on a course for the Capital," said the sailor.

Chapter 4

The Capital

alwin had heard about the Capital all his life, a magnificent city of marble palaces and hanging gardens. He had trouble believing the stories. Yet Lieutenant Gavin and Sergeant Hitch, as well as the sailors aboard ship, had all been there, and they talked about it as if it was a real place. He couldn't wait to see it for himself.

They kept sailing south, beyond the islands he knew, passing larger islands he'd never been to. Two days into the voyage, the peak of a mountain showed above the horizon. Soon after, more peaks appeared. Within a few hours, Halwin could tell that the bases of the mountains touched, forming a single large island. The flatlands around them were covered with fields and pastures. Every harbor and crossroad had its own village or town.

As they drew closer, the white towers and domes of the Capital became visible from the sea. The walls could have circled Outermost Island and still had room for the reefs and kelp beds and reefs surrounding it.

"Do you see that golden dome halfway up the slope?" The sailor pointed to a formal-looking structure that glittered in the sunlight. "That's the Temple where the priests offer prayers and sacrifices to the Holy Ones. On certain days of the year, like the winter solstice, people from the most powerful families in the city are allowed inside to watch."

Halwin thought of the charms he spoke during a normal day, and the burnt offerings he made at the hearth on special occasions. The grandeur of the Temple made him feel like a barefoot rustic with no education. That's what he was, but he'd never been self-conscious about it before.

The sailor pointed to a walled compound of mansions and towers at the foot of a mountain. "Do you see that terrace, the one with palm trees in the garden? That's part of a courtyard inside the Palace." Halwin stared at the ponds and fountains. He hadn't known such places existed.

They tacked to enter the harbor. At least a hundred ships lay at anchor, most of them larger than their own vessel. They changed course again and again to thread between them.

Sailors climbed into the rigging. They dropped the sails, and clouds of linen descended from the masts and billowed to the deck. Someone threw a rope to a boat in which two oarsmen manned every oar, and it towed them to the wharf.

Along the wharf was a stone quay where a dozen ocean-going vessels could tie up at once. Almost every space was occupied. They tied up at the only empty space and lowered the gangplank. A middle-aged man with iron grey hair waited at its foot.

"I am Sergeant Hitch. I will train you, and I will lead you into battle," he said in the language of the Capital.

From almost the moment they left the ship, they began training for war. Sergeant Hitch arranged them into ranks. In ranks of six across, the column of new recruits marched behind him to the barracks. They were required to speak the language of the Capital, even in private conversation among themselves. It was awkward. Halwin struggled to translate in his head.

The next morning, Lieutenant Gavin gathered all the squads under his command. He looked them over as if addressing each man individually.

"Men, when you complete your training, you'll be sent to the Mainland. There, you will drive the enemy warlord from the grain-growing region."

Lieutenant Gavin waited until the murmuring died down.

"Our survival depends on these food shipments. Twenty years ago, when we signed the trade agreement, King Turstan married one of the Caliph's daughters as a gesture of friendship between our two nations."

In the days that followed, their training began in earnest. One day was much like another. They were taught how to use a spear, they drilled on the parade ground, and they learned the habit of instant obedience.

A few weeks after they arrived, Sergeant Hitch handed Cuinn a letter from home. He broke the seal, and a grin spread across his face. "I'm a father, I have a son!" For the rest of the day, he kept pulling out the letter and reading it again, smiling to himself.

The recruits learned to fight in formation, to raise a shield wall, and to recognize the commands sounded by the horn. Every waking moment was taken up with training, and they saw nothing of the city beyond the barracks and the parade ground.

A few months later, when spring arrived, and the seawater grew warm, Sergeant Hitch pronounced their training complete. Halwin felt they'd barely mastered the basics, but time was pressing, they had a war to fight. Everyone in the squad was issued a chain mail shirt, helmet, and a blue tabard bearing the royal badge, a ship under full sail under a golden crown. Halwin and his fellow islanders were men-at-arms now, and ready to go to war.

That afternoon, Lieutenant Gavin summoned the men to hear an announcement. When they gathered at the assembly area, the Lieutenant was standing with a man dressed in plain robes of grey and brown, but even more finely made than what aristocrats usually wore. The Lieutenant introduced the visitor as an adviser to King Turstan, a royal minister in the diplomatic corps.

"In a few days, you'll sail for the Mainland," said the Minister. "You'll march to the region where our grain is grown and drive out the sorcerer warlord."

"After the warlord is defeated, we must continue to defend our source of wheat, oats, and barley. King Turstan has decided we should occupy the area and form a permanent settlement. Thus, those of you who choose to stay on the Mainland with the occupation will receive farms of your own."

Halwin shifted uneasily. "Are we rescuing our closest ally, or invading them?" he asked Ulrich. "Because it sounds like we're planning to colonize lands we don't own."

Cuinn, on the other hand, grinned from ear to ear. "Now I know how we'll manage, what with the new baby. This couldn't have come at a better time."

The following day, Lieutenant Gavin interrupted one of Sergeant Hitch's drills and pulled Halwin out of the line. "I need streamers for the tips of the lances. Go to the marketplace and get a fathom each of blue, green, and purple silk. Find something light enough to float on the wind."

Halwin leapt at the chance. In all these months, he hadn't been to the city at all, he hadn't even had a chance to visit the taverns on the waterfront.

The market was a short distance from the parade ground. Halwin found it easily. It was so crowded, he had to dodge around people. More than once, someone shoved an elbow in his ribs. He hadn't experienced crowding like that before. His heart pounded, and he fought the impulse to flee to the safety of the barracks.

Every booth held an array of luxury goods, goblets with jewels around the rim, gaming boards of rare woods with ivory inlay, beautiful shoes that couldn't possibly be comfortable to wear, bright colored birds in cages, small wooden caskets painted by artists. Whatever it was, there was no scarcity of it. The sight of so many costly, impractical things left Halwin cold. *There's nothing here anyone actually needs.*

With time and patience, and by pushing through the people around him, Halwin made it into the textiles part of the market. He found a silk vendor and picked out fabric for streamers in blue, purple, and green. The merchant measured out a fathom of each and gave him a little extra.

Halwin hadn't seen any food for sale except for roasted meat on a skewer, sold to be eaten while walking around the marketplace. There were no displays of bread, eggs, or flour. No fish. No live chickens.

There were sounds of a scuffle in the far corner of the market. Someone shouted in a way that suggested blood was about to be shed. Several women pleaded with him to calm down.

The area where the shouts were coming from was fenced off, and two sentries guarded the entrance. A long line of people waited to get in. Someone left carrying a green glass bottle and a small canvas sack, and the sentries allowed the next person in line to enter.

Halwin could see into the enclosed area. Sacks of grain were stacked chest high. Nearby, a white awning covered a table piled with fish, mussels, and an octopus.

One stall over, there were pottery jars of the sort used to store cooking oil.

"But I want to buy a full measure." A woman's voice climbed in pitch with frustration.

"I can only sell half a measure per customer, that's the law," said the man tending the booth.

People outside the entrance started pushing and shoving. Armed guards rushed over to help the sentries. The crowd pressed in. Halwin found himself getting shoved repeatedly. Someone shoved him. He fell to his knees, and his bundle of silk hit the paving stones. He scooped it up and struggled to his feet. A bell tolled, and someone with a low, booming voice ordered people to disperse and return to their own homes. Clutching his silk, Halwin fled from the marketplace.

Back at the barracks, Halwin and his squad mates watched a column of smoke rising from among the merchants' stalls.

Halwin was dismayed. "What was all that about?" he asked Sergeant Hitch.

"Bread riots. They happen all the time, now that the fish have disappeared."

The next morning, they carried barrels, tent canvas, and wagon wheels up the gangplank into the belly of the ship. Halwin made trip after trip, but couldn't seem to make a dent in the piles of foodstuffs and gear piled up on the quay.

Supplies arrived from the warehouses as fast as they could stow them.

Once, he and Cuinn carried a large wooden chest into the hold, one of them grasping the rope handles at each end. Walking backward, Halwin missed his footing and almost stepped over the edge. It made him acutely aware of how narrow the plank was, and how it moved as the ship rocked on the swell.

Lieutenant Gavin led a stallion up the narrow walkway. Halwin paused to watch, the weight of the sack of barley pressing hard on his shoulder. A narrow bridge with water on either side should scare a horse, but the large bay seemed to take it in stride. More horses were led onto the ship, and they climbed the gangplank just as calmly. Apparently, warhorses were hard to scare.

"Halwin, don't just stand and stare," said the Sergeant. "The fleet is sailing on the turn of tide. That's in less than an hour. If there's a sack of oats or bundle of spears sitting on the quay when the signal comes, we're leaving without it."

A short time later, every foot soldier in the squad, as well as their officers, boarded the enormous warship.

"This is it, men. Take a good look at Armelos, it may be your last for quite some time," said Sergeant Hitch.

Chapter 5

Burnt Cottage

he voyage to the Mainland took five days. The great ship left the harbor with the rest of the fleet and sailed east, leaving the island kingdom behind. In the lee of the main island, the waves were small and choppy. Light air gusted from all directions. Once they reached the open ocean, they caught the wind that blew steadily from the west. Within a few hours, the peaks of Armelos sank beneath the horizon and disappeared. Only the line where the sky met the blue-purple ocean remained.

Halwin had never been out of sight of land before. He didn't particularly like it. He was overwhelmed by the immeasurable size of the ocean, but at the same time, he couldn't leave the ship. He felt trapped.

Halwin had another worry. The ocean was so vast. Once the war was over, and those who didn't want to stay returned home, how would they find their islands in the middle of a trackless ocean? What if they sailed right past them? At some point, they'd reach the ends of the earth. He imagined an immense waterfall spilling seawater over the edge of the world. The current would sweep them away before there was time to turn back. Cuinn touched his arm.

"Halwin, you're looking a little green. Don't stare at your feet. Look at the horizon and you'll feel better."

When Halwin came up on deck the next morning, there was still no sign of land. The wind blew steadily from the west.

Waves rolled up from behind them, lifting their stern. Halwin and the rest of his squad sat on deck in the shade of one of the sails. The breeze freshened, and the ship heeled over and hissed through the sea. It was a restful afternoon until Lieutenant Gavin wandered over and began to quiz them.

"Who knows why we're going to the Mainland?" he asked.

"To drive off the warlord who seized the grain lands for himself," said Halwin.

"What will happen if we fail?"

"Our families will starve," said Alaric, the red-headed youth from Ulrich's village.

"And what do we know about this warlord?" asked the Lieutenant.

The men looked at each other, then looked back at him.

"That is correct. We know almost nothing," he said. "Lord Zuriel came out of nowhere. We don't know who his father was, or where he was born, or even his real name. 'Zuriel' sounds like the name of one of the Holy Ones. Most likely he started using it to make himself seem more important."

After three days out of sight of land, the surface of the sea took on the blue-green hue of shallow water. Everything to the east seemed to have increased in height and roughness. Within hours, the Mainland filled the eastern horizon.

They approached the coast and turned north, keeping well offshore.

"We're not going to land here?" asked Halwin.

"No, It's too shallow for a ship our size. We'd scrape our keel on the bottom and get stuck before we got anywhere near shore," said the sailor.

The Mainland was mostly desert. There were no harbors or mouths of rivers which would allow a fleet of warships to land. On the second day, they turned toward shore, moving fast with the full force of the breeze in their sails. Ahead of them, the surf broke against the base of rocky cliffs with a booming sound, sending tall white plumes into the air.

Halwin looked at the sailors, who didn't appear to be concerned.

"That's our inlet," said the sailor. "Welcome to Deepharbor, the only port on the coast that can handle a warship this size."

Behind them, the rest of the fleet had also tacked and were moving toward the inlet.

The ship entered a narrow inlet flanked on both sides by sheer faces of rock which towered above the masts of their vessels and reduced the sky to a thin strip of blue. They seemed to tip together, squeezing the narrow space. Halwin's ship was more than halfway down when the last of the fleet entered the inlet. The hundreds of ships were dwarfed beneath the cliffs.

Sergeant Hitch put his fingers between his teeth and whistled to summon the squad. "Every man needs to suit up. That means leather armor, chain mail hauberk, and weapons. When we land, we might meet some resistance from the locals. Don't worry about it. A determined show of force will send them running."

Halwin's ship was the first to make landfall, and his squad one of the first ashore. The longboats carried them through the surf. At one point, the swell threatened to swamp the boat. Halwin clutched the gunwales. His pulse raced. He was a strong swimmer, but a shirt of chain mail could pull anyone to the bottom.

The breeze from shore carried the aroma of mudflats, a mixture of rotting seaweed and dead fish. The prow of the longboat scraped bottom, and Halwin waded through the surf clutching his spear and pack. He struggled through the stinking mud to reach the loose sand above the high tide mark, where the others had already begun to form up in a defensive formation. The wind sighed through the beach grasses, but except for seabirds, there was no other sound. Sergeant Hitch scanned the terrain and motioned them to stay alert.

A row of heads appeared above the dunes. A band of tribesmen descended on the soldiers of Armelos, shrieking and swinging ragged-looking scimitars. Tattoos covered their foreheads and cheeks, and their teeth had been filed to points. Halwin's squad formed a shield wall and assumed a wedge formation. They plowed through the middle of the attacking horde. The first few tribesmen went down, and the others fled, abandoning the bodies of the fallen.

After the battle, the squad assembled near the longboats at the edge of the mudflats. All up and down the beach, other units were returning from the skirmish. Late in the afternoon, the light began to fade. They lit a fire of driftwood to drive off the gnats and sat close to it, cleaning their weapons.

"Well, if that's what battle's like, I feel ready to take on the sorcerer warlord," Halwin announced.

"That was just a skirmish. We're about to face the entire host of Lord Zuriel," said Sergeant Hitch.

The next morning, the army of Armelos began the long trek inland. Desert gave way to grasslands and small stands of trees. The sky was clear and blue. Halwin shivered in the chill of early spring and wrapped his cloak more tightly around himself.

They marched six abreast along an endless road through forests and grasslands. Fields newly plowed for spring planting hugged the wide gravel pavement on both sides. Wildflowers grew on the shoulder, purple and white. Halwin didn't know their names. They didn't grow in the unforgiving soil on Outermost Island.

The road plunged into the woods. Above the treetops, a column of smoke rose in the still air, acrid and stinging. Halwin wiped his eyes on the back of his sleeve, careful not to scratch himself on the rings of his chain mail.

They rounded a bend. Beside the road was what, until recently, had been a farm family's home. The stone walls rose as high as a man's shoulder, but the thatch and the timbers supporting it had collapsed into the space they enclosed. Blackened remnants of straw and wood still smoldered. Here and there, a cinder glowed orange.

"We're too late. It looks like the enemy got here before us," said Sergeant Hitch.

"Their army has been through already?" asked Cuinn.

"The main body of their army is still to the south. I'm guessing this was done by scouts sent in advance of the main army," said the Sergeant.

Primitive-looking arrows stuck in the ground, bristling like the spines of a hedgehog. Another had pierced the trunk of a tree just behind the cottage. Halwin pulled an arrow from the dirt. Its ragged feathers were as black as a raven's. He was about to touch the barbed tip when Sergeant Hitch said, "Drop it. That's an ouphe arrow. It might be poisoned." Halwin lobbed the evil-looking thing into the bushes.

"Awf?" he asked.

"Ouphe," said Sergeant Hitch. "A hellion or goblin. Smarter than most, and more aggressive. It's said they make up much of Lord Zuriel's army."

Halwin felt ill. Since no one said otherwise, he'd expected the enemy to be much like the tribesmen they'd defeated at Deepharbor, men with tattooed faces and teeth filed to points. He hadn't signed up to fight monsters.

Against the shattered walls, the beginnings of a vegetable garden were starting to come up. The cabbages were still too young to pick, but the little bean plants were almost knee high. Some careful householder had tied them to poles with string. They hung limp and withered from the fire.

Halwin shrank back. The site might be infested with haunts, those lonely and unhappy spirits who'd died wrongly, or too soon. He made a warding sign against the evil eye, his first and little fingers forming the horns. Alaric did the same, and so did Brennan.

Sergeant Hitch approached the soot-blackened structure. He stepped within the ruined walls, then turned away, retching. His face was grey and sweat beaded on his forehead. Halwin craned his neck and almost broke rank, but the Sergeant waved him back. "Nothing to see. Get back in line."

They left the ruined cottage and marched down the road through woodlands and fields. Each step closed the distance between themselves and the enemy. Halwin swallowed hard, his mouth dry.

They marched for a mile or so in silence. Halwin turned to Cuinn, who was marching beside him. "I thought the warlord came from the east, a month's travel from here. Why do you suppose he's coming here now?"

Cuinn considered the question. "Maybe there were too many of them for the land to support, and then they had a crop failure. Same reason we're here."

In the rank ahead of them, Alaric said to Ulrich, "I've heard that ouphe are short and hunchbacked, with grey-green skin and claws like iron nails. The older ones, whose fur has gone silver, have the curved tusks of a wild boar." Reddish curls stuck out beneath Alaric's helm, and the armor made for a grown man overwhelmed his slender frame.

Halwin had heard worse. Ouphe weren't human, and they ate the flesh of men. He didn't know what the Sergeant had seen in the burnt cottage, but is must have been bad.

"They say the Ouphe are like wild dogs," said Ulrich, the largest and most formidable warrior in the squad. "They're too disorganized to work together. They can't even do simple maneuvers like form a shield wall." Hador, a silent brute almost as large as Ulrich, nodded.

"No one knows how the warlord controls them," said Cuinn.

"That Lord Zuriel must be a regular demon," said Halwin.

Lieutenant Gavin reined in beside them and glared down at Halwin.

"Don't say demon," said the Lieutenant. "The Fallen are still counted among the Holy Ones, even though they've committed crimes and are no longer blessèd."

"I didn't mean a real one. We were talking about the enemy warlord."

Lieutenant Gavin rode off, and Halwin said, "I didn't know the Lieutenant was religious."

"Everyone's religious before a battle," said Cuinn. "But once the fighting starts, he'll be swearing in the names of the Holy Ones just like everyone else."

Further ahead, they passed through a tiny village where every house was shuttered and dark. Behind one of the windows, a curtain twitched and then fell back into place. Other than that, the village might have been abandoned. Even the animals had vanished.

Lieutenant Gavin galloped down the column, followed by a standard bearer with the Lieutenant's personal device, a Moray eel baring its teeth. The wind freshened, and the bottle-green silk streamed behind him. In a short time, Sergeant Hitch's squad, and all the other squads under Lieutenant Gavin's command would follow that standard into battle.

"This is it, men. Our scouts sighted the enemy army, just over the next hill," said the Lieutenant.

A chill ran through Halwin's body, beyond the damp and fresh air of the morning. His metal armor seemed to pull the heat from his body, even through the padded gambeson. He realized his hands were shaking.

Chapter 6

First Sight of the Enemy

he drumbeat quickened. Halwin and his friends stepped up their pace. They were about to confront the enemy. Halwin put a hand in his pocket. His fingers brushed against the little pebble he'd picked up on the beach the morning he left Outermost Island. It was something from home, and its smooth surface gave him comfort. He'd give anything to be back at his own cottage right now, even to do least-loved chores like mucking out the pigpen. He vowed to return the pebble to the spot where he'd found it. It would be a charm to get him home safely, too.

Pipes and horns joined the drums. The music stirred his blood. Halwin marched a little faster, more eager than afraid.

They rounded the crest of the hill, and the trumpet called a halt. The landscape opened up before them. Halwin jostled to see around the men in front of him.

The road descended a grassy slope to a stone bridge barely wide enough for a farmer's wagon, but sturdy and solid. The water was running high from the spring rains. It flowed briskly, making whitecaps where it spilled over the boulders.

On the far side of the bridge, the road passed through a broad plain of farmland and disappeared into the woods beyond. And there, on the plain beyond the river, the host of the enemy lay waiting for them, a dark-colored mass that glittered where the sun reflected from thousands of helms and edged weapons.

The trees blocked all sight of the horizon, but about the treetops, a line of squalls could be seen moving in from the south.

"I don't like the looks of that weather," said Halwin. "It makes the back of my neck prickle. Do you suppose it's the work of that sorcerer warlord?"

"If you saw something like that at sea," said Sergeant Hitch. "You'd think nothing of it. You'd just shorten sail and ride it out."

"That may be, but it still makes me uneasy," Halwin said under his breath.

The host of the enemy was arranged in rectangular formations that seemed to go on forever. Individual units clustered around the standards of their captains, and there were scores of standards, hundreds, even.

The Lieutenant's jaw dropped. "Their army is twice the size of ours."

"But we have the uphill advantage," said Sergeant Hitch.

"It's not enough." The Lieutenant spoke so softly, that even though Halwin was close enough to touch the Lieutenant's stirruped foot, he wasn't sure he'd heard correctly.

Enemy soldiers continued to pour from the woods. They marched in ranks of ten, overflowing the road and trampling the farmland on either side. "Hail Zuriel!" Their war cry carried to the top of the ridge where Halwin stood watching in horror.

The dark-clad warriors formed up into small blocks. They stood around for a time before joining the main formation. Once they were in position, the next unit moved.

"They're being moved like the stones on a game board. It's like they're under the control of a single mind," said Halwin. "Do you think the warlord is controlling them with sorcery?"

"He's controlling them, but I expect it's in the usual way, through their officers," said Sergeant Hitch.

"An inexperienced general might think central command is a good idea," said Lieutenant Gavin. "And it is, until something unexpected happens. It's very hard to get new orders to the captains fast enough."

"Why haven't they taken the bridge?" asked Sergeant Hitch. "Doesn't the first army to arrive always take the bridge?"

"Maybe it's because they're closer than we are, and they'll capture it when we start to advance down the slope," said Lieutenant Gavin.

"Or maybe they're idiots," said Sergeant Hitch.

The line of clouds moved up from the south, eroding the blue sky overhead. Their shadow crept across the host of the enemy, snuffing the sunlight twinkling from their weapons and making the generally dark color of their clothing appear black and ominous. Halwin and his squad watched from the sunlit ridge, where the light looked golden compared with the darkness on the other side of the river.

A distant rumbling came from the direction of the storm front, and the air felt heavy and oppressive. The wind freshened. Silk pennants lifted from their poles and snapped in the breeze.

The cloud was low and fast-moving. Its underside looked greenish in color, and it moved like a living thing. Nothing about it looked natural. Halwin frowned at the sky, and the hairs on the back of his neck prickled.

Trumpets sounded up and down the ridge, and the men formed into a line that stretched the entire length of the ridge, in ranks four and five deep. The General rode up on an enormous white horse, its harness glinting in the sun. His standard, a silver ship on a dark blue background, caught the breeze and filled like a sail, confident and proud. They reined in less than twenty paces away. Halwin lowered his eyes, suddenly shy. General Olwen was an exalted man. Not only did he command the entire invasion force, but he'd married into the royal family as well.

The horn sounded Attention, and the standard bearer said, "General Olwen will address the troops." The buzz of conversation faded away, leaving only the scolding of blue jays and the trill of frogs. The General stood in the stirrups and pulled off his helm. A scar ran across his cheek, and his iron-grey hair and beard were clipped short, the image of a professional soldier. The General began to speak. His voice carried over the men like the call of the trumpet.

"Before us lies the host of the enemy."

He gestured to the far side of the river where enemy soldiers were still emerging from the woods, chanting their harsh-sounding battle cries.

"You are the most highly trained and disciplined force on earth. Let no man underestimate how dangerous we are…"

Enemy troops, who'd shown no interest in the bridge until now, broke loose from the enemy host and sprinted for the stone footing on the far bank.

"Take the bridge!" shouted the General.

Chapter 7

The Battle at Stone Bridge

he enemy runners were only a hundred strides from the bridge. Halwin raced down the slope, dropping his pack and bedroll. The stems of wildflowers slapped against his legs, and a cloud of locusts rose from the tall grasses with a sort of musical hum. He clutched his spear in both hands, and his leather breastplate clattered against the chain mail.

A hail of arrows from the far bank hung in the air and began to descend. There was nothing he could do about them. He kept sprinting for the bridge. They struck the ground all around him, hundreds of them, each one like the ragged, evil-looking bolt at the burnt cottage he'd flung aside when he'd thought it might be poisoned.

Halwin's squad would be the first to reach the bridge. It would be up to them to hold off the creatures until the others arrived. He labored for breath even though he was running downhill.

The first few runners from the enemy army reached the far end of the bridge and began to cross. They swept over the arch and kept going, their misshapen forms dark against the pale stone. Strange designs decorated their shields, and they brandished curved blades that were hooked at the end. Their bodies looked twisted, as if something had broken and never healed right, and the hands that gripped their weapons were the claws of monsters.

They must not reach the near bank. The bridge was twenty paces ahead. Ten paces. He was almost there.

For such stoop-postured, shambling creatures, the Ouphe moved with surprising speed. Halwin made it to the foot of the bridge moments before they did. As long as his squad held them off, the enemy couldn't cross.

Halwin and the other men advanced on the ouphes, their spears bristling before them. Halwin had never seen an ouphe up close before. A horned helmet covered most of its face, and its ragged chain mail hung in shreds. Through the eye slits, its skin looked greenish-grey, and its chin was marked with ritual scars. He threatened it with his spear, and it pulled back its lip in a snarl, revealing its fangs.

The men pushed forward and forced the ouphes to retreat. They recovered within a few steps and lunged forward again. A creature with a short sword struck the shaft of Halwin's spear, but the sturdy ashwood held up. Halwin tried to return the blow, but Cuinn was pressed against him so tightly, he couldn't lift his arm.

In the center of the bridge, an ouphe commander stood on the rail and barked an order which cut short when a pale-colored arrow struck him in the throat. He clawed at it and staggered against the parapet, then overbalanced and plunged into the water. The weight of his armor dragged him under, and a trail of bubbles above the spot where he fell drifted away on the current.

So many ouphes were struck by pale arrows, bodies blocked the roadbed. Their fellows dragged them to the side and dumped them into the river.

A solid mass of Ouphe swarmed over the stone arch. When they reached the end, they pushed Halwin's squad back, off the bridge and onto the riverbank.

Just before the squad was surrounded, Sergeant Hitch ordered them to fall back. They retreated up the hill and made it to the wall of kite-shaped shields, each bearing the royal badge of Armelos. One of the shield bearers opened a gap just wide enough to let Halwin and the rest of his unit slip through.

With five ranks of men and a shield wall between him and the Ouphe, Halwin was able to catch his breath for the first time since he charged down the slope. His whole body shook. Sweat soaked his tunic beneath the gambeson, in spite of the chill of the day. Small scratches and cuts he hadn't noticed before began to sting.

The wind picked up, and the greenish overcast overtook them, covering the sun. Wisps broke loose and reformed in a way that seemed deliberate. It was only mid-afternoon, but the gloom made it feel like twilight.

Someone shrieked a cry of warning. The men in front lifted their shields. Arrows thumped into the wood with a hollow sound like a drum. Someone down the line fell to the ground, screaming. Halwin's heart hammered, and he couldn't breathe. If the attention of one of the foot soldiers holding the shields wandered, or a stray arrow managed to get past him, Halwin could die. There wasn't a thing he could do about it. He began to shake uncontrollably, and something warm soaked the inside of his leggings.

A thick column of enemy foot soldiers and horsemen funneled across the bridge, fanning out along the near bank and assembling in well-ordered blocks behind individual standards.

An even greater number were attempting to ford the river itself. Black-armored ouphes waded through the reeds in water little deeper than their knees, then struggled through the water.

Those that reached the near side clambered up the riverbank, a thicket of brambles and saplings, and joined the rapidly growing formations. The enemy line grew to ten ranks deep. The enemy kept coming, spilling out of the woods and streaming across the river.

The soldiers of the enemy began to march up the slope, their tattered black standards streaming in the wind. In spite of their unruly appearance, their line was perfectly even.

The drums beat a slow, steady rhythm, a deep rumble felt in the bones, menacing and unstoppable. "Hail Zuriel!" they chanted in low, guttural voices. It sounded like glass breaking.

In the midst of all the noise and confusion, the Captain's warhorse seemed calm. Halwin had thought horses were nervous animals, but the big stallion seemed to take the chaos of battle in stride.

Enemy arrows flew from their archers' position on the near bank. They struck the ground in front of the advancing enemy troops, who marched through the deadly barrage without slowing down. Nor did the enemy archers lower their bows. They brought down at least a dozen of their countrymen, who collapsed and lay motionless on the hillside while their comrades stepped over their bodies. Halwin shook his head in disbelief. If they were controlled by a single mind, their master's attention appeared to be elsewhere.

The enemy continued to march up the hill. Halwin left his position of safety at the rear of the formation. Clutching the shaft of his spear, he took up a position immediately behind the shield wall. Individual ouphes were visible in the gap between shields. One wore scaled armor and carried an axe. Another was covered with spines, its cheek pulled back by a ring that pierced the skin.

They waited for the command to advance. The enemy was twenty paces away, so close the wind carried the smell of them, a mixture of unwashed clothing and privies. Still, the order didn't come.

"The waiting is the hardest part," the Sergeant said.

The standards of the Ouphe, tattered black fabric painted with harsh designs, jolted with each step as their bearers marched up the slope.

The trumpet sounded, "To arms!"

"That's our call. Move out, men," the Sergeant ordered. "And whatever you do, don't break rank."

Lieutenant Gavin's standard, the green panel bearing a Moray eel, began to move down the hill. The whole line followed behind it. Halwin tried to step forward, but his feet were anchored to the ground. Without comment, Sergeant Hitch shoved him between the shoulders to propel him forward.

The dark-colored horde surged at them like an incoming tide. The distance between the two armies closed until Halwin could hear their breathing and the rattle of their armor.

The lines collided. With a great clash, the Ouphe struck the shield wall with their weapons, shrieking their terrifying battle cries. Halwin's heart hammered, but hours of drill took over, and he didn't have to think. Choose a target, step forward, thrust. Twist the spear free and strike again. Swords rang against swords, spears stuck leather cuirasses, and maces thudded onto wooden shields. A swing of a mace found its mark, and someone screamed.

An ouphe in leather armor lifted a jagged scimitar. Beneath the helm, its grey skin was covered in tattoos. Halwin aimed a spear thrust at its belly, but the ouphe parried it with a blow from the scimitar that made Halwin's palms sting. An axe struck his shoulder. The chain mail held, but the force of it drove the rings into his flesh.

An enemy's scimitar shattered Halwin's spear and left the ashwood shaft in splinters. One of their own men lay on the ground near Halwin's feet. The corpse's fingers gripped an undamaged spear, red with the owner's blood. Halwin bent to pick it up A blow to his helm knocked him to his knees. It hurt, and the ringing almost deafened him. An ouphe stood on the shaft of the spear Halwin was trying to grasp. It was lifting a heavy war hammer, preparing to strike the blow that would finish him off.

The Ouphe had taken staggering losses. Their twisted bodies littered the hillside. Armelos' line had thinned so much, glimpses of the river showed between them. Halwin allowed himself a moment of satisfaction. Armelos was winning.

Lieutenant Gavin galloped over, looking agitated. His standard bearer was with him, and the bottle-green panel flapped over their heads.

"They're stretching their line. They're trying to flank us. Stretch match them," said the Lieutenant.

"Everyone spread out. Ranks in back, move forward," ordered the Sergeant. The gaps between shields grew wider.

Halwin stood with the others in his squad, holding back the ouphe with their spears. His arms shook from exhaustion. Normally he would have been relieved by now, but there was no one behind him.

The Lieutenant thundered up, flecks of foam flying from his stallion's mouth. "See that rock? Stretch the line to reach it." A natural outcropping of rock protruded from the hill, achingly close. If they could anchor against it, the enemy couldn't flank them.

"Impossible. We're one deep," said the Sergeant.

"It's a bad situation, but getting flanked is worse," said the Lieutenant.

They spread out as much as they dared. The rock was ten paces away, but they couldn't stretch any more. Ouphes started to swarm around the end of Armelos' line. The green banner with the Moray eel wavered and fell over.

"Hinge! Fold the line and back up the hill," ordered the Sergeant. His voice was tight. Hinging was an act of desperation to delay the inevitable.

Halwin marched backwards up the slope, reluctant to lose the ground they'd fought for. He stumbled over a body and barely kept his balance. A mass of ouphes swarmed between Halwin and the wall of rock they'd failed to reach.

A blow landed on his arm which ached like bee stings. Blood soaked his sleeve, and the stain widened with every heartbeat. He gripped his spear with one hand, his injured arm hanging useless. His vision narrowed to a small circle, and the din of battle roared around him. Halwin resolved to fight until he dropped from exhaustion, or until he was cut down.

Just then, a cheer rose from the end of the line. And they were human voices, not ouphe.

Chapter 8

The Rout

The enemy line broke up, and the Ouphe began fighting as individuals. Their superior numbers were almost useless against Armelos' formations and tactics.

Lieutenant Gavin galloped over and reined in. He and his standard bearer looked bedraggled, and muddy footprints ran across the green silk panel.

"I could hardly believe my eyes," said the Lieutenant. "Their line just fell apart, as if they were under a spell, and the spell wore off. I never saw anything like it."

An ouphe left the melee and ran toward the river. Several others followed. One by one, the entire horde broke away from the fighting and fled.

"After them!" said Sergeant Hitch.

Halwin and his squad chased the deserters down the slope. The first of them struggled through the underbrush, then waded into the water. Some found rocks to step on or shallow places to wade across. Others entered chest deep water that soon reached over their heads. One slipped and fell, then sank from the weight of his own armor and disappeared beneath the surface.

Halwin pushed through the thicket that grew on the bank. The riverbank was higher than a man was tall. There was no easy path through the brambles, and he struggled to keep his footing on the slick mud. Sergeant Hitch led them into the water. Halwin followed. Water poured into his boots, cold enough to made his skin tingle.

They scrambled across the ford, yelling threats and insults at the enemy, and chasing them before the tips of their spears.

In the center of the river, Halwin slipped on an algae-covered stone and fell into water deeper than his head. The weight of his chain mail dragged him below the surface. He tried to scream and breathed in a lungful of water. A strong hand grabbed him and lifted him out of the water. Hador, one of the largest men in the squad. Halwin sputtered his thanks. The big man only nodded.

The enemy continued to fall back. The men of Armelos pursued them, but while the army of Armelos was still fording the river, the Ouphe reached the opposite bank and took off running.

Halwin's squad made it to the shallows on the far side and forced their way through the reeds and cattails to the gravel shore. Enemy soldiers were fleeing for the trees. Soaking wet, Halwin sprinted after them, the front of his tabard flapping wetly against his legs.

The road was littered with their helmets and shields as if the enemy had dropped everything that might slow their flight.

Halwin's armor was heavy, and he could only run so far. Breathless, he slowed to a trot. Their squad wasn't the first to give chase. Every once in a while, Halwin saw remnants of the Ouphe army, individuals or small bands, but when they approached, the creatures took off running.

Halwin's squad hurried through the woods and emerged in the grasslands on the far side. Soon they passed the baggage wagons which had been at the rear of the enemy army. Now they stood abandoned, the oxen grazing in the traces.

Bodies of the dead and wounded lay in the road and in the fields on either side. They must have been cut down when the army of Armelos overtook the warlord's defeated legions. In the plowed farmland, a creature Halwin had taken for dead reared up and grabbed him by the ankle. Halwin drove a spear between the chinks in its armor.

Hoofbeats shook the ground. Halwin looked up. Half a
dozen riders, all in black, flew down the road. A banner
bearing the enemy warlord's device, the symbol for Earth
twisted into the symbol for Fire, streamed above their heads.

A wedge-shaped formation of warriors in silver armor on
pale horses bore down on them. The standard-bearer carried a
blue panel bearing a ship under full sail, General Olwen's
personal device.

"Lord Zuriel, you are a coward!" General Olwen shook his
fist at the backs of the fleeing horsemen.

Halwin looked up, the creature dying at the end of his
spear momentarily forgotten. The largest of the black horsemen
reined in and whirled around to face the General.

"What did you call me?" His voice was low and harsh. He
spurred his black stallion forward, and his sword came out of
the scabbard with a hiss. Behind him, his companions melted
into the chaos of the rout, apparently unaware their leader was
no longer with them.

General Olwen sat in the saddle, the reins loose in his
hands. He made no move for the hilt of his own sword.

"You flatter yourself to think I'd duel with you as an equal.
You're nothing more than a thug with an army."

Beneath the helm, the warlord's mouth twisted in
contempt. "I will annihilate you." He advanced with the
confidence of one who has an army at his back.

The horses of the General's men danced around,
whinnying, as their riders fought for control. Only the
General's mount remained still, beyond a twitch that rippled up
its haunches.

"Look behind you," said the General.

The warlord hesitated, then turned to look over his
shoulder. Shields and weapons littered the ground where his
people had dropped them. Other than that, the road was
empty. So were the surrounding fields. The warlord's arm froze
in mid-gesture.

General Olwen laughed, then nodded to Lieutenant Gavin.
"Take him."

Halwin's squad closed in around the enemy warlord. He fought fiercely. The arc of his sword took out several good men, even though its range was less than that of the spears. When a man fell, another rushed in to take his place. It could only end one way. The warlord was outnumbered, and foot soldiers were closing in on him from all sides.

To his credit, he was a fighter. He parried most of the spear thrusts, and the rest glanced harmlessly off his armor. Then Ulrich, a huge man of enormous strength, landed a blow that sliced the warlord's leg just above the knee. Blood soaked his clothing and ran down the apron of his saddle. His sword arm faltered in mid-swing. Someone darted in and cut the girth, and a dozen hands pulled the warlord from the saddle. He hit the ground and lay on his back with the wind knocked out, gasping like a fish.

The threatening overcast that had hung over the battlefield all day broke up and was carried away. Dappled sunlight broke through the clouds for the first time since the fighting began.

Beneath the helm, the warlord's unremarkable features were framed by reddish-brown hair. It was the face of a man. Halwin was disappointed. He'd expected the enemy leader to be even more of a monster than the creatures he commanded.

The warlord's sword lay on the ground by his hand. He reached for it, but as his fingers closed on the grip, Hador's boot came down on his wrist. The man's eyes widened and he cursed under his breath.

Brennan came running over. "Alaric is dead!" Alaric, the red-headed farm boy, had been the first to reach the warlord, and the first to be cut down.

Ulrich looked stricken. "Alaric's from my village. I promised his folks I'd keep him safe." His eyes swam, and a vein throbbed in his neck. Ulrich walked up to the fallen warlord and leaned over him. The prisoner tried to twist free, but his arm was still pinned under Hador's boot.

"This is for Alaric!" Ulrich leaned over the warlord and spat on him. The glob ran down the side of his neck. Then Ulrich pulled back his foot and kicked the warlord in the ribs, hard. Something cracked. The prisoner fell back and lay still, breathing in shallow, panting breaths. Blood from the wound in his leg soaked the ground beneath him.

They all jumped in, hitting and punching. "Bastard!" "Murderer!" The frenzy overtook him. Halwin kicked the prisoner over and over until someone grabbed him and dragged him back.

"That's enough," said Sergeant Hitch. The circle of men pulled away, grumbling, like a pack of dogs deprived of their prey.

The prisoner lay in the dirt, blood flowing from his nose and mouth. A captive should have looked scared or possibly withdrawn beyond reach into his own head. But the warlord's eyes were those of a predator: *I'm planning something, and you're not going to like it.* Halwin's skin crawled.

Lieutenant Gavin trotted over. He could barely control his pale-colored stallion. It danced sideways, tossing its head and showing the whites of its eyes. The Lieutenant tried to soothe the animal, then swung a leg over the saddle and dropped to the ground.

The warlord started to lift his head, but the Lieutenant pressed the tip of his sword under his chin. "One move and you're a dead man. Do you understand me?" The sword tip dimpled the skin, and a pinprick of blood appeared. There was a long pause before the prisoner nodded almost imperceptibly, a single dip of the chin.

The Lieutenant turned to the largest and strongest of the foot soldiers. "Strip him of armor and weapons, then bind his hands. We'll figure out what to do with him when we get back to camp."

Chapter 9

Guard Duty

verything's under control. We don't need help."
Lieutenant Gavin shooed away a lieutenant from another unit.
Halwin understood why. A captured enemy leader was a
trophy which reflected great glory on the units that captured
him. The Lieutenant wasn't about to share that glory with
another officer. "Hitch, find something to use as a stretcher.
There's no way he can walk," he said. "And send over your
strongest men. Dismiss the rest."

The line of slow-moving carts had only just caught up with
them. They left the road and headed for a grassy area not far
from the battlefield, where they formed up in a large circle.

"Men, follow the baggage wagons and set up camp," said
Sergeant Hitch. "After you finish, you're at liberty for the rest
of the afternoon."

Halwin and his squad mates hiked across the meadow,
stirring up grasshoppers and cicadas as they pushed through
the tall grasses. He felt jubilant about winning the battle and
still being alive to walk in the sunlight, but almost too tired to
enjoy it.

They pushed between a small gap between the head of one
cart and the tail of another to reach the protected space within.

"The battle's won. I don't see why we're still sheltering
behind the wagons," said Halwin.

"The worst dangers are the ones you don't see coming," said Cuinn. "There might be a few ouphes still around, or wild animals we don't know about."

The cart carrying their squad's gear had their squad's number painted on its side, so they had no trouble finding it. They worked in silence. They'd done this so often, there was no need to speak. Halwin carried tent canvas, pounded stakes into the ground, and, with his good arm, helped to drag the last wooden chest from the wagon bed. When they finished, a sentry climbed up in the empty wagon bed and looked out over the empty grasslands, where crows settled on the bodies of the dead. The sentry leaned on his spear, looking bored.

Small encampments were going up all around them. The squads who'd been their immediate neighbors the move before, and the move before that, were still camped beside them, lugging wooden chests and rolls of canvas to the area around their own fire pits. Off in the distance, in the center of camp, the Command tent were being raised, the tallest structure in camp. Pennants of blue and purple silk streamed from its twin peaks.

Someone brought over an armload of firewood and struck a spark to it. A wisp of smoke rose from the shavings. Flames sprang up, and sap popped in the dry branches. Halwin sank to the ground and slumped against a wagon wheel. His eyes closed, and his wounded arm throbbed.

"Before you nod off, let me clean that cut for you," said Brennan.

Brennan knelt in front of him with a tin basin and a sponge. Halwin bit his lip against the sting of lye soap while his squad mate cleaned out the deep cut on his arm. When it was over, Halwin let out a breath of relief. He opened his eyes. Brennan was threading a curved needle about the size of a scythe blade.

"You are not going to use that on me." Halwin backed into the wagon wheel behind him and tried to squeeze between the spokes.

"Don't be such a baby," said Brennan. "You act like you've never let your mother remove a sliver."

Brennan worked quickly. He tied off the last knot and wrapped a long strip of linen around Halwin's arm. He tied it off and handed Halwin a dipper of water to drink. It tasted like the bottom of a chicken coop. Halwin gagged and spit it out.

"The well water around here tastes of iron," said Brennan. "But after you've lived here for a while, you won't even notice."

"I haven't decided whether I want to stay," said Halwin.

"There's time to think about it. Those returning to Armelos won't pack up and leave just yet." Brennan punched Halwin on the shoulder. "In the meantime, don't get into any fights during the victory celebrations and pull out the stitches."

Of course there would be victory celebrations, for those that could stay awake. At the camps of some of the neighboring squads, the drinking had already started. Someone was singing verses from a well-known drinking song and botching the words. In the aftermath of battle, he was suddenly exhausted. It was all he could do to keep his eyes open.

Sergeant Hitch entered their encampment, and the men chanted, "The Sergeant led us to victory. Huzzah, huzzah!"

"This victory is yours." The Sergeant held up an unusually large bottle of wine. "Pass this around. Don't feel you need to hold back, there's plenty more where it came from."

The men sat around the fire, sitting on barrels and crates, talking about the battle.

"How did we win?" asked Halwin. "They outnumbered us two to one."

"They had to fight uphill," said Ulrich.

"We had the uphill advantage, but it wasn't enough. The warlord should have won." Sergeant Hitch looked into the flames and furrowed his brow. "I don't think their commander knew what he was doing."

Lieutenant Gavin entered the encampment. "Sergeant Perenn sent his men to guard the prisoner so your men can have a break."

Sergeant Hitch got to his feet. "We captured the warlord, so by rights, we're the ones guarding him. I won't have Perenn grabbing glory he didn't earn."

"That's what I thought you'd say. But you'd better move fast, or Perenn will steal your trophy," said the Lieutenant.

Sergeant Hitch studied the soldiers nodding around the fire. "I need two men for guard duty."

"So he doesn't escape?" asked Ulrich.

"So no other squad shows up and tries to take the credit," said the Sergeant.

"The prisoner makes my skin crawl," Halwin said to Cuinn. "I don't want to go anywhere near him."

"Halwin, you were talking when you should have been listening," said the Sergeant. "That just earned you a shift of guard duty. Cuinn, you can keep him company."

What a waste of a rare afternoon off. With a sigh, Halwin resigned himself to a long and boring shift. He'd miss the time at liberty the rest of his squad was enjoying. Worse, he'd miss the feasting and drinking that evening to celebrate their victory.

Grumbling, Halwin got to his feet. He put his arms in the sleeves of his hauberk and let the chain mail shirt slide around him. One of the rings caught in his hair. He cursed and tugged it loose. He strapped on a breastplate of hardened leather and straightened his helm, then chose a spear from the rack while he waited for Cuinn to finish lacing up his bracers.

When they finished suiting up, Halwin followed Sergeant Hitch, with Cuinn right behind him.

They threaded among the closely spaced tents toward the center of camp, navigating by the pennants flying from the twin peaks of the Command tent, silken streamers of blue and green, the colors of the sea.

Off-duty soldiers, stacks of shields and weapons, and the occasional chicken jammed the dusty footpaths between tents. Here and there, snatches of song reached him. Everyone seemed to be in a holiday mood, even those with an arm in a sling or a bandage around his head.

The close-packed tents gave way to an open space used as a parade ground. The Command tent stood in the center of camp, towering above its neighbors.

In the middle of the parade ground, workmen stacked planks next to four stakes driven into the ground. Another one sawed out the notched sides for a low set of stairs. From the area defined by the four stakes and its location near the

General's tent, it appeared they were building a stage. The General must be getting ready to make an announcement. Halwin hoped he would tell them to pack up and board the ships for home.

Sergeant Hitch led them to a crowded area at the side of the parade ground and stopped in front of a large tent of the sort used to store supplies. No pennant flew from its peak, and no standard stood beside its door. Like almost every other tent in camp, it was a single-pole pavilion. But unlike the others, it was ringed by a dozen foot men-at-arms in chain mail hauberks and steel helms, each of them heavily armed.

"He's being held in a supply tent? Not a brig?" asked Halwin.

"Look around you. This is a military camp. There's nothing but tents," said the Sergeant.

They approached the entrance. The tent flap moved, and a soldier from another squad stormed out, making the sign of the evil eye.

"That's it. I'm not standing guard in here again."

The soldier who'd shared the duty with him looked just as rattled. Halwin watched them hurry away.

"What was that about?" Halwin asked.

"There's a rumor going around that the prisoner can look into your eyes and steal your soul, or some such nonsense," said Sergeant Hitch, rolling his eyes.

Halwin wondered if his own squad had started the rumor, to scare the other squads away.

Sergeant Hitch continued. "Now, about guard duty. All you have to do is watch the prisoner. He probably won't say anything. He hasn't opened his mouth since he was captured. Even the interrogators couldn't get a word out of him. And don't get too close to him. He's restrained, but even so, keep a distance of at least a fathom or more."

"Because of the evil eye?" asked Halwin.

"Because you might get spit on or kicked," said the Sergeant. He lifted the tent flap and motioned them to follow.

Chapter 10 Homesickness

alwin and Cuinn followed Sergeant Hitch into the supply tent. Inside, sacks of flour were piled high, forming a wall. A wagon wheel leaned against them, and wooden crates were stacked nearby.

The prisoner was sitting on the ground, leaning against the center pole with his arms behind his back. His chin rested on his chest, and his face was hidden under the hood of a dark green cloak. One knee was bent, and the other leg was stretched out before him. His feet were bare, and a chain connected the irons around his ankles. A rust-colored smudge across the ball of his foot surrounded what looked like a deep cut. He must have stepped on a rock after they'd stripped him of shoes and weapons.

The gash above his knee where the spearhead had sliced it open hadn't been bandaged or even washed. The wound was caked in dried blood, rust-colored against his skin. The fabric around it had dried into stiff, sharp-edged wrinkles. Fresh blood beaded up along the edge of the wound. He moved as if he couldn't get comfortable, and his breathing was ragged.

Sergeant Hitch stood well away from the prisoner. "There he is. Lord Zuriel, the dreaded warlord. Not so proud now, are you?"

The prisoner stirred, and the chains made a clinking sound. He lifted his head. The hood of his cloak fell back, revealing a

48

purple bruise around his eye and a cut lip so swollen, it distorted his features. He regarded Halwin the way a predator studies its prey, its eyes impersonal and calculating. Halwin looked at the prisoner's shoulder, taking great care to avoid his eyes.

"Should we have someone in to patch him up?" asked Cuinn.

"No, we have wounded of our own. They need to be seen first."

The Sergeant started to duck under the tent flap. "One more thing. If he gives you any trouble, just shout. A dozen spearmen outside will come to your aid."

Once the Sergeant had gone, Halwin and Cuinn took up their positions inside the tent, one on either side of the door. They leaned on their spears and settled in for a long watch.

An hour crept by. The prisoner moved from time to time as if unable to get comfortable. His cloak slipped and fell between his back and the tent pole. He looked up as if he expected one of them to get it for him. Halwin pretended not to notice. After a while, he drew his knees to his chest and hunched over, shivering.

They weren't supposed to talk in front of the prisoner, but Halwin assumed that meant in a widely spoken language. Speaking in the dialect of the outer islands, Halwin said to Cuinn, "Our officer said our guest has no military talent whatsoever."

The prisoner's head snapped up. He glared at Halwin through narrowed eyes. For a moment, Halwin thought the prisoner had understood him. Impossible. No more than a hundred people spoke the outer islands' language, and Halwin knew them all by sight. "Our officer also said our guest claims to be great among the casters of spells. However, our guest is known to take the truth and improve it, so there's little chance he can actually work spells."

The prisoner tapped his foot like a cat lashing its tail back and forth when it's annoyed.

Halwin leaned in his spear. His feet hurt. The nicks and bruises from fighting hurt. The fatigue that follows battle had set in, and he wanted nothing so much as to lie down and sleep. The prisoner, on the other hand, was sitting up straight and moving as if he was no longer injured. Halwin frowned. He'd been seriously wounded in battle and then beaten half to death. Yet in just a few hours, he'd gotten better.

The sound of hammering reached them from the direction of the Command tent. The prisoner's head snapped around, and his whole body stiffened. Somebody was building something. This was an army camp. Somebody was always building something. Halwin couldn't understand why it seemed to upset the prisoner so much.

Inside the tent, the linen walls turned dull and grey.

"That strange green overcast is back," said one of the spearmen outside. "I hate how you can't see the weather here until it's right on top of you. Now at home, you can look out to sea and know what's coming. The storms can't sneak up on you."

"Do you know what I miss?" said his partner, "The colors of the sea. Here, everything is tawny grasses and green woodlands. It doesn't look right."

Halwin was starting to feel homesick himself. Now that they'd won the battle, he wanted to know how when they would march to the coast and board the ships that would take them home.

Just recently, he'd heard more talk of settling here and farming than of sailing for home. It made him anxious.

He couldn't wait to be home. He'd tell his brothers and sisters all about the Capital, and the battle, and everything he'd seen on the endless Mainland. And more than he liked to admit, he missed his dog. He touched the pebble in his pocket, his good luck charm, the only thing he had from home.

And there was a girl, Elinn. In his mind, her linen dress hugged her figure as she bent to pick the blue-purple wildflowers that grew between the rocks. The wind from the ocean stirred her hair. He'd never told her he loved her. Regret hit him like a punch in the gut. He had to get back home. He had to see he again.

"Did I ever mention how I felt about Elinn?" Halwin asked Cuinn.

"On occasion. You said she had no meat on her bones, and she looked like a horseshoe crab with an overbite," said Cuinn.

Halwin remembered saying those things, but he couldn't remember why. His cheeks burned.

"And besides, she's spoken for," said Cuinn. "She and the Holbeck boy have had an understanding since they were small."

Halwin knew that. He ignored his friend. He loved Elinn. He would find a way to return to the storm-swept island where they both had been born, and he would ask her to marry him.

The army would march back to Deepharbor. There, they'd meet the ships that would carry them to Armelos. From the Capital, he'd catch one of the trading vessels that plied the outer islands. It would carry him to Outermost island on the northernmost tip of the island chain. Beyond it, there was nothing but a blue-purple horizon, the endless sweep of the sea.

Cuinn smiled to himself. "I was just thinking about how nice it would be to have my own farm here. I'd get established here and then sent for my family. I can see myself plowing the rich black earth beneath these grasslands. And at the end of a long day in the fields, I'll go back to our cabin, to my wife and baby."

The prisoner stared at Cuinn. He mouthed some words but made no sound. Cuinn shifted from foot to foot, breathing like someone who was badly frightened.

"I saw myself going home, and found our cabin in ruins, like the burnt cottage we passed this morning." Cuinn stared into the distance. His eyes were haunted. "I don't think I want to stay here and farm, after all."

Halwin glanced at the prisoner. The corner of his mouth curled in a smirk.

Chapter 11

Possession

ithout meaning to, Halwin looked directly at the prisoner's face. Their eyes locked, and Halwin felt something brush against his mind. It fingered his thoughts and left him feeling unclean, as if he'd been contaminated. From the corner of his eye, he saw the prisoner's mouth twist into a half smile. Halwin couldn't prove it, but he knew, he just knew, that the prisoner was doing something to him.

"Stop it!" Repulsed, Halwin jerked away. Cuinn looked at him questioningly.

Halwin fought against the tendrils that dug into his mind like the roots of a tree. He focused on the runes scratched into a side of a wooden crate. Speaking each letter aloud, he sounded out the words for "honey" and "dried peas." It didn't help. The probing touch was still there.

Anxiety swept over him. What if the ship never made it to Armelos? He knew what the sea could do to a fragile fishing craft, but he'd never thought twice about going to sea in an ocean-going vessel. In his mind's eye, he was standing on deck watching the shores of the Mainland disappear in their wake. Storm clouds were building on the horizon. In his imaginings, he knew something no one else on board knew, that within the hour, the ship would be lost with all hands. He tried to warn the others, but his voice was gone, and his feet were rooted to the deck.

Outside the tent, the wind picked up. The torches wavered and grew dim, then sprang up and burned brightly. Sudden droplets of rain stuck the tent canvas like a handful of pebbles. The linen fabric of the tent billowed like a sail, and the hard-packed earth seemed to tip. Halyards slapped against the mast, and the salt spray felt fresh and clean against his face. The rough planks of the deck were coarse beneath his toes, and seawater foamed icy cold against his bare feet and ankles. Halwin looked down. He was still wearing boots.

The tent canvas glowed golden in the torchlight from outside. Beyond it, a line of squalls was moving in fast. The wind picked up, and the sails filled with a crack. Huge waves towered over the ship, higher than the top of the mast. The deck heeled over until the gunwales hissed through the surf.

A wave towering over them crested and broke. Whitewater foamed down its sides. The decks amidships drowned beneath the surf. Icy water knocked Halwin off his feet, then swept him along the deck and over the rail. He kicked for the surface, but a wave broke over his head, making him sputter and cough.

On the other side of the linen wall, the Sergeant gave routine orders to one of the spearmen. Their shadows wavered against the tent canvas, the outlines tall and distorted.

Green water surrounded him, and bubbles rose among the ribbons of kelp. Light from the surface receded to a bright circle, like the view from the bottom of a well.

And then he saw them. *Nymphs!* Their hair floated around them like seaweed. Their eyes were flat and cold, and their cheeks puffed like those of a Moray eel, revealing tiny, coral-sharp teeth.

A clammy arm shot out. Unnaturally long fingers with claws like scythes reached for his face. Halwin screamed, and his lungs filled with seawater. His fingers found the dagger at his belt. He pulled it loose and struck. The arm yanked back, and the blow slashed across its ribs. The creature screamed.

There was a crash outside on the parade ground, like the hull of a ship splintering on the rocks. Someone cursed, and someone else shouted. The greenish underwater light vanished and took the kelp forest with it.

The prisoner gasped and jerked his head in the direction of the noise. He recovered almost right away and assumed a look of boredom.

Halwin blinked. Cuinn was backing away from him, his eyes wide. "By the Gods, have your wits deserted you?"

A slash in the front of Cuinn's tabard gaped open, revealing a deep scratch across the leather armor. Mortified, Halwin returned his dagger back to its sheath. The prisoner looked at Halwin and smirked.

The feathery touch returned. Strands of kelp floated in the green water. Halwin had a great sense of danger, and his hand moved for the hilt of his dagger.

"No!" Halwin plunged out of the tent.

Outside, he stood with the spearmen guarding the door, trying to decide what to do. His hands shook, and he clenched them to steady himself. He'd just left his post, a serious breach of discipline. He'd left Cuinn was alone inside with whatever that thing was. He should go back. He said to the first spearman he saw, "Brennan, will you relieve me for a few minutes?"

Brennan hesitated, then lifted the tent flap while making the sign of the evil eye. *That won't be enough.*

Chapter 12 **The Stables**

alwin stood outside the tent. The western horizon glowed purple with the last of the sunset, but the rest of the sky was covered. The overcast blocked the stars, and a misting rain chilled his face.

He was sure, absolutely sure, the prisoner was using magic on them. Worse, he'd just learned the prisoner had the power to make one soldier attack another. Halwin hated to leave Cuinn with the sorcerer, but his friend might be in greater danger if Halwin stayed with him. He said to one of the spearmen, "I need to find Sergeant Hitch," and set off for their encampment at a run.

Twilight had come early, and the light was grey. The sky looked much as it had over the battlefield that morning, low and fast-moving. It was unnatural-looking, and it felt oppressive.

In front of the Command tent, several long poles lay jumbled together. They must have fallen and made that enormous crash that had woken him from that nightmare vision of drowning.

It was a fair distance from the center of camp to the place where his squad had their tents and campfire. Halwin hurried in that direction to look for Sergeant Hitch. He wove between the tents, jumping over tent ropes and dodging around wagons.

He passed the encampments of other units, each one a small cluster of tents arranged around a fire pit. He expected to hear the singing and loud talk from the victory celebrations he regretted missing, but the camp was unexpectedly quiet. Here and there, fragments of conversation reached him as he threaded around barrels and pack animals.

"I'm afraid to drink the water here. It tastes like it's been poisoned."

"You're not used to it."

"No, it's more than that. I've never had water that tastes this bad. Maybe there are still a few Ouphe around, and they've gotten into the wells."

Further along, two burly men, one with a bandage over his eye, unloaded firewood from a cart. It blocked the path, and Halwin had to slow down to squeeze around it.

"I don't think the officers have our backs. They sit on their horses in the safety of the rear and order us into the fray," said one of them.

"It's easy to them to throw away our lives. Most of them don't even know our names," said the other.

Soon after, Halwin reached the place where his own squad was camped, just inside the barricade of baggage wagons. The Sergeant wasn't there.

Halwin had never seen so many long faces. After an astonishing victory like today's, the men should have been celebrating. Instead, they were sitting around with slumped shoulders, griping.

"Do you know what I think? The officers lured us here with the promise of our own farms, but they want us for serfs on their estates. I saw myself walking behind the plow, wearing rags and a thrall collar around my neck. No thank you. Not after I was promised a small plot of my own."

"The sooner we march for the ships, the better."

"Where's Sergeant Hitch?" Halwin asked.

"He's looking for the Lieutenant," said one of the soldiers. "Try the stables. Gavin is like all the officers. He cares about the horses more than the men."

Halwin went back toward the center of camp. It was dark, and the misty rain soaked his clothing.

The stable tent was unusually large, with multiple peaks. Pieces of straw littered the ground around it and it smelled strongly of horses. As he entered the stables, Halwin rehearsed what he wanted to say. *The prisoner is using magic on me. He made me attack Cuinn. He's more dangerous than we realized.*

Halwin stood in the shadows of the entrance, waiting to be noticed. A hoof stamped the hard ground, and there was a low snort, but other than that, the horses were quiet. It was after dark. Probably most of them were asleep.

The voices of Sergeant Hitch and Lieutenant Gavin came from within.

"I left to check on the wounded," said Sergeant Hitch. "When I came back, the men fell silent. Most of them turned away. One of them laughed."

"When was this?" asked Lieutenant Gavin, stroking the neck of his pale-colored stallion.

"Right around the time that unnatural-looking overcast returned. Losing the sun seemed to turn them surly."

A horse neighed loudly. Another echoed it.

The Lieutenant lowered his voice. "There's an ugly mood sweeping through camp. It's not just the men who are unhappy. Some of the captains have stopped trusting General Olwen. There's talk of having him removed."

The horse was strangely uneasy, tossing his head and rolling his eyes. Other horses in the stables tent were just as restless, whinnying and stamping their feet.

"We were supposed to go home after the battle," said Lieutenant Gavin, "But now the General's saying we're to stay here and start a colony."

That's been the plan all along. Yet the Sergeant was nodding along with him. He was acting as if his own memory had failed as completely as the Lieutenant's.

Lieutenant Gavin's stallion reared up and fought against the halter. With great difficulty, the Lieutenant quieted it, but twitches still ran up and down its flanks.

"I don't know what's gotten into them. You'd think there was a snake in the straw," he said.

Lieutenant Gavin had spoken open rebellion. Halwin's mouth went dry. He backed away as quietly as he could, then waited until the Sergeant left the stables on his own.

Sergeant Hitch looked at him sharply. "Halwin, why did you leave your post?"

Halwin flushed, but he didn't back down. "The prisoner is more dangerous than we knew. He bespelled me and made me attack Cuinn."

"Halwin, nobody used magic on you. You need to return to your post."

Inside the stables, the whinnying of the horses reached a frantic level.

At that moment, he knew. Zuriel was using magic to poison men's minds. The horses felt it, too.

"Sergeant Hitch, I need to tell you..."

"Return to your post. And let's have no more talk of magic."

"But..."

"Halwin, that was an order." The Sergeant pointed to the door.

With a growing sense of dread, Halwin slipped out into the night and rain.

Chapter 13

An Unfamiliar Soldier

t was fully dark outside, It was fully dark outside, and Halwin found it hard to see. Torches and wood-burning in iron braziers provided most of the light. A raindrop struck his wrist, and then another. Halwin felt completely dejected. The warlord had possessed him and tried to make him hurt Cuinn. He'd managed to escape and ask the Sergeant for help, but the Sergeant hadn't believed him

He reached into his pocket for the little pebble from the beach at home. His fingers closed on cloth. The pebble wasn't there. He'd begun to think of it as a charm that to him home safely, and the loss of it troubled him greatly.

The wind picked up. The gusts almost blew out the torches, reducing the flames to wavering and almost unreadable shadows. Halwin picked his way around the ropes holding up a tent, then tripped over the rails of a handcart he couldn't see in the dark.

Across the parade ground, the Command tent glowed yellow from the lamplight within. Workmen silhouetted against its linen walls struggled to raise a tripod-like structure over the wooden stage. A block-and-tackle hung below the point where the poles met. It looked like a gin, the makeshift crane sailors used to lift cargo from the hull of a ship. Once it was up, the hammering started again.

It wasn't a gin, it was a gallows. Halwin's gut wrenched. He'd never seen a gallows before, and it filled him with dread. They were going to hang the prisoner. No wonder the sound of hammering had upset him so much.

Space had opened up around the tent where the prisoner was being held. Since he'd been gone, some of the neighbors pulled up stakes and left. At the edge of the trampled grass, another tent was being taken down. The white canvas lay on the ground like a jellyfish washed up on the beach. Soldiers carried away cots and sea chests in the rain, at an hour when they normally would have been asleep. Halwin didn't blame them for leaving. The sorcerer warlord made his skin crawl, too.

The two largest men in the squad, Ulrich and Hador, flanked the entrance to the tent. Halwin nodded a greeting and accepted a spear from Ulrich. He swallowed hard, then lifted the tent flap and went in.

The ground at the door was slick with mud. Inside, the rain drummed against the canvas. Brennan looked deeply relieved to see him. He left more quickly than was polite.

The prisoner was slumped against the base of the center pole. His head rested on his knees, and his cloak lay behind him. Halwin was careful not to look directly at him for fear of getting being possessed again.

The rust-colored smear still covered the ball of the prisoner's foot but the deep cut wasn't there anymore. Halwin risked a sideways glance at their captive's face. The black eye had faded to yellow-green, and the cut on his lip was gone. It wasn't natural. No one heals that fast. It might be a trick of the light, or perhaps he remembered wrong. Either way, it left him feeling uneasy.

Something fingered the surface of Halwin's mind. He shook his head to drive it off. It didn't help. Tendrils probed until they found a way in. The ground tipped beneath his feet, and the supplies stacked in the back of the tent seemed to waver as if seen through the hot air of a fire. *It's not fair. I didn't even look at him.*

Cuinn was spreading an oilcloth over the sacks of grain to keep water from dripping on them. He saw Halwin and waved a greeting.

Something stirred in the shadows. An enormous black dog moved with incredible speed and knocked Cuinn to the ground. Not a dog, a wolf. An unusually dark one with a few strands of silver in its coat. Cuinn screamed. Cuinn tried to fight it off, but it seized his throat and silenced him.

Halwin reached his friend in a few long strides, gripping his spear. He sank the steel tip deep into the wolf's shoulder. Wounded, the beast lifted its injured foreleg and bared its teeth, but it didn't back off. Halwin struck again. The spearhead sank between the animal's ribs and the creature collapsed. Halwin stabbed it over and over to be sure he'd pierced its heart. Twitches ran up its legs, and it lay still.

Another large animal growled behind him. Halwin wheeled around. A second beast, the color of saddle leather and leaner than the first, crouched as if ready to spring. Halwin gripped his spear and braced himself for the impact. It hesitated as if trying to decide what to do, and Halwin stabbed it in the neck. The creature yelped and sank to the ground, bleeding from the nose and mouth. It whimpered once, then sighed as the life left its body.

A whole pack poured into the tent. *They'll have to go through me to reach Cuinn.* They closed in, growling and snapping. Halwin aimed his spear to keep the lot of them at bay and drive them away from Cuinn, lying motionless on the ground.

A well-placed jab brought down one of the wolves, but the motion ripped out the stitches above Halwin's wrist. The reopened wound stung fiercely. Blood soaked the linen bandages.

The spear stuck in the dead wolf's body. Halwin tugged the shaft to free it, but the spearhead was caught on something. He tried to twist it loose. While he struggled, another wolf clamped its jaws on his wrist. Halwin kicked the animal in the ribs. It released his arm but left the tracks of its teeth in his flesh. With a tremendous pull, Halwin wrenched the spearhead from between its ribs. Halwin shook with fatigue. He knew that if he tripped or stumbled, the wolves would finish him.

The flap at the entrance was pushed aside. An enormous wolf entered the tent, the largest he'd seen so far. Muscles rippled beneath its iron-grey fur, and it moved with a self-assurance the younger wolves lacked.

The old wolf advanced on Halwin, purposeful and grim. The others sprang aside to let it through. A low rumble emerged from its throat, and the hackles rose along its spine. Halwin felt sure this one meant to kill him. He waited until it was almost upon him, then stabbed at its heart. It dodged the thrust with the ease of an experienced warrior. He tried again, but only left a bloody scratch on the creature's muzzle. *All I've done is make it mad.*

The grey wolf would beat him handily, without even trying very hard. Halwin's pulse hammered in his ears. He backed away. Something caught him behind the ankles. The spear flew out of his hands and clattered to the ground. He fell and struck his head.

When he came to, the tendrils in his mind were gone and the voices of his squad mates surrounded him. He whispered a prayer of deliverance.

"Ulrich and Hador, pin his arms," said Sergeant Hitch.

"You're not going to finish him off?" asked Ulrich.

"I would have, but he knocked himself out first," said the Sergeant.

The point of a spear was shoved in Halwin's face. At the far end of the shaft were the hands of the man who held it. Sergeant Hitch. The bridge of his nose bled from a scratch. The Sergeant's grey hair showed beneath his helmet, and his eyes were merciless. Halwin lay perfectly still, hardly daring to breathe.

"Someone find me some cord." The Sergeant's voice was cold. Two men pressed Halwin's shoulders into the ground with more force than necessary. He felt every one of the cuts from the battle that morning and from fighting off the wolves.

Near the entrance, soldiers were tending the wounded and covering the faces of the dead. In the spot where the second wolf had fallen, Brennan lay on his back with his eyes closed. His lips were blue. One of the men covered his face with a cloak. They moved like soldiers walking the battlefield after the battle was over, studying the ground at their feet, not on the alert for danger. Halwin looked around. The wolves were gone.

"Someone check on Cuinn," said the Sergeant.

A soldier walked past Halwin and knelt. Halwin twisted in the grip of the strong men holding him down and craned his neck to see. The soldier wet a finger and held it before Cuinn's mouth, then shook his head. He covered Cuinn's face with a cloak.

"No! You'll smother him." Halwin broke free of his captors and yanked the cloak from Cuinn's face.

Cuinn lay on his back, staring at the canvas above him with unblinking eyes. The ground beneath him was dark with blood. His skin was the color of a fish's underbelly, and his lips were blue. A spear wound sliced his upper arm. Another pierced his leather armor, going deep into the gut. Halwin touched his friend's hand. It was already beginning to cool. Cuinn was dead. Halwin wailed, a high-pitched, keening cry.

There were no bite marks on Cuinn's neck, even though Halwin had watched a wolf tear out his throat. Halwin looked around. Three of his squad mates lay dead, and as many were wounded. The ground should have been littered with the bodies of wolves, but there were none.

A roaring filled his ears like the gale force winds of a line of squalls before they hit. There had never been any wolves. The sorcerer had put the vision in his head, and he'd fallen for it. Cuinn was dead, and Halwin had killed him. Halwin slumped forward and covered his face with his hands.

"Seize him and bind his hands," the Sergeant ordered.

Strong arms grabbed him from behind and pulled him off of Cuinn's body. Sick with remorse, Halwin didn't resist them. They pulled his arms behind his back and bound his wrists so tightly, the cords cut into his skin. They finished tightening the knots and left him lying on his face.

"Why do you think he went mad?" Ulrich was talking about Halwin rather than to him, even though he was right there.

"The whole camp's gone mad," said the Sergeant. "We hanged an entire squad for mutiny. Unrelated to that, General Olwen's second-in-command started a rival faction and tried to have him removed. The army's falling apart, for no reason. This land must be cursed."

Halwin's eyes widened. Lord Zuriel couldn't defeat the army of Armelos on the field of battle. But with sorcery, he could destroy it from within. He was unimaginably dangerous.

"Sergeant Hitch?" said Halwin. "The warlord is causing the ugly mood sweeping through camp. He's trying to make the invasion force fall apart."

"Silence!" The Sergeant pressed the tip of his spear into Halwin's throat. Halwin shrank from the steel point, not daring to breathe.

"But..." Halwin said.

"Gag him," said the Sergeant. "I don't need to listen to the ravings of a madman. No sorcerer has that kind of power."

Ulrich tore a strip of cloth from Halwin's tabard and stuffed it in his mouth. Halwin tried to spit it out, but couldn't.

The ground was damp from the rain. It chilled his cheek and soaked into the front of his clothing. Halwin understood why the warlord wanted to collapse the invasion force, but why make Halwin kill his friends? *Unless...*

Halwin lifted his head to look at the warlord. At the base of the tent pole, the green cloak lay on the ground where it had fallen earlier. Links of chain lay scattered around it, broken and twisted. The iron fetters had not so much been opened as exploded. The prisoner was gone.

Nearby, a soldier leaned on his spear and watched them with detachment. He wore the same sort of tabard and chain mail as any other man-at-arms. At first, Halwin mistook him for Alaric, the boy killed during the capture. The unfamiliar soldier had the same reddish-brown hair, but he looked older, and his eyes were cold and mocking.

A metal cuff encircled the stranger's wrist. A few links of chain hung from it. The man bent the thick band of iron between his fingers until it broke, then dropped the fragments to the ground. He picked up the cloak beside the tent pole, then looked around to see that he was unobserved.

With studied casualness, the stranger strolled toward the tent flap. He walked with a slight limp as if there was a stone in his shoe. His boots left the prints of bare feet in the mud at the entrance, the outlines of heel and toes clearly visible.

Lord Zuriel! That's him, he's getting away. Halwin fought against the bonds and tried to shout a warning through the gag. His words were unintelligible.

"What's going to happen to him?" asked Ulrich.

"The Lieutenant will decide, but I expect he's the hangman's problem now," said Sergeant Hitch.

Halwin's blood ran cold. He fought like a crazed thing, but the bonds held. He wasn't going home. He'd never give a silver chain to a girl, and he'd never pet his dog again.

Outside, the noise and commotion had drawn a crowd. Soldiers, looking as if they'd been roused from their beds, stood ten deep around the tent. Some had pulled on their boots over bare legs, and the shirts they'd slept in stuck to their skin in the rain.

Lord Zuriel stepped through the tent flap. He shifted his spear from one shoulder to the other, then melted into the crowd outside. The spear, like the pole of a standard, should have shown exactly where he was in the throng, but no shaft stood above the press of men, and no spearhead glinted in the torchlight. He was simply gone.

EARTH

FIRE

EARTH AND FIRE

www.FallenWarlord.com

If you enjoyed this story, please visit the website for free
samples from the Fallen Warlord series.

Acknowledgements

I wish to thank everyone who helped me produce this story by brainstorming and critiquing the various parts week after week. In particular, I wish to thank the members of the Loudoun County Writers Group, the Reston Writers' Review, and the Loudoun County Science Fiction and Fantasy group, also known as the Hourlings. (motto - "A rising tide floats all boats.")

Billy Aguiar, Don Anderson, Paul Bourgeois, Bob Dillon, John Dwight, Peter Dube, Jr., Martin Berman-Gorvine, Erica Gravely, Jeremy Holloway, Jeffrey C. Jacobs, Christopher James, Jessica Johnson, David Keener, Bill Krieger, Jennifer Loizeaux, Erin Ljungdahl, Gordon McFarland, Shea Megale, Micah, Jeff Patterson, Jon Payne, Rachael, Katharine Reed, Donna Royston, Rin Sanders, Adam Shannon, Matt Shea, Tyson Warren, Martin Wilsey, and Jason Winn

With special thanks to:

Jeremy Holloway for sharing his experiences in Afghanistan and telling me what real soldiers would have done.

John Dwight for beta reading and coming up with the ending.

Jessica Johnson for developmental editing, bringing a special gift for pacing.

Donna Royston for line and developmental editing, and for her extensive knowledge about literature.

Peter Dube, Jr. for lending his artist's eye to the design of the cover.

Martin Wilsey for figuring out the world of independent publishing, and more importantly, for bringing the rest of us along with him.

About the Author

Liz Hayes is an engineer by inclination and training. She began her career at Jet Propulsion Labs, and later moved east to be an analyst and statistician for the Federal Government.

She's fascinated by medieval reenactment, and writes LOTR fanfiction under the penname Uvatha the Horseman. While doing the research for a fanfic about Sauron forging the Ring, she joined the local guild and became an amateur blacksmith herself. It's an excellent hobby which combines her two favorite things, craft projects and pyromania.

She lives in Northern Virginia with her husband and three teenage children she keeps in line by threatening to show up at PTA meetings in full Jedi robes.

Other books by Liz Hayes

Tannhauser Press brings you...

TANNHAUSER PRESS

TANNHAUSERPRESS.COM

www.ingramcontent.com/pod-product-compliance
Lightning Source LLC
Chambersburg PA
CBHW020643130626
46552CB00003B/1383